My First
ELMER
Joke Book

A Red Fox Book

Published by Random House Children's Books
20 Vauxhall Bridge Road, London SW1V 2SA

A division of The Random House Group Ltd
London Melbourne Sydney Auckland
Johannesburg and agencies throughout the world

Text and illustrations © David McKee 2000

3 5 7 9 10 8 6 4

Printed in Hong Kong
THE RANDOM HOUSE GROUP Limited Reg. No. 954009

ISBN 0 09 940406 0

My First ELMER Joke Book

David McKee

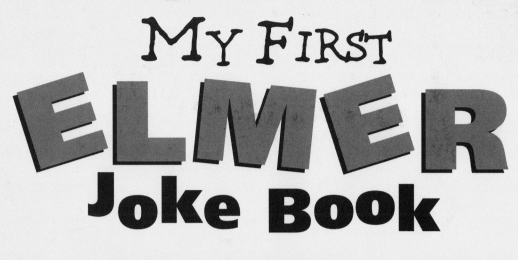

RED FOX

What do you call a **big** grey wobbly animal with a trunk?

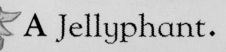

A Jellyphant.

How do you greet
Elmer on stilts?

High!

 **What's grey and has a big trunk?**
A mouse going on holiday.

What's grey and has two trunks?
An elephant going on holiday.

 What do animals eat on the beach?
Sandwiches.

Why did Elmer wear sunglasses?
Because he didn't want to be recognised.

How do you know that elephants like swimming?
They've always got their trunks with them.

Why do elephants have trunks?
Because they'd look silly in bikinis!

What do kangaroos
wear in winter?
Jumpers.

What do Elmer and his
friends sing at Christmas?
'Jungle bells, Jungle bells.'

What do you
call an elephant
at the North Pole?
Lost.

What keys have fur?
Monkeys.

**What do you call a crocodile
with no teeth?**
Anything you like, it can't bite.

Why was Elmer's teddy cold?
Because it was
a little bear.

What animals always forget?
Owls – they're always saying,
'Who? Who?'

**What do elephants say when
their children are naughty?**
'Tusk, tusk!'

What do you give an
elephant with **big** feet?

Plenty of room.

What is the **biggest**
insect in the world?
An eleph-ant.

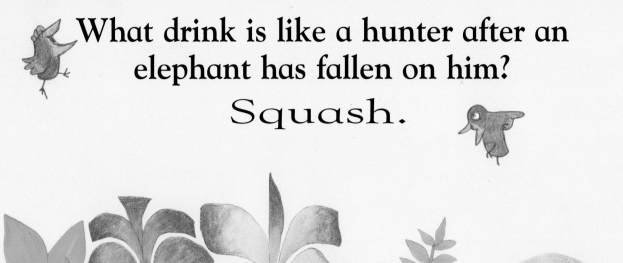

What drink is like a hunter after an
elephant has fallen on him?
Squash.

Why do giraffes have such long necks?

To join their heads to their bodies.

What is a snake's
favourite lesson?
Sssspelling.

Why can't you play
jokes on snakes?
Because you can
never pull their leg.

 What do you call elephants that
stand in the rain and laugh?
Wet.

**What do you call an elephant
with no teeth?**
Gumbo.

What do you call a
flying elephant?
A jumbo jet.

Where can you buy a
second-hand elephant?
At a jumbo sale.

What goes black, white, *ouch*,
black, white, *ouch*?

Wilbur rolling down a hill!

When does Elmer eat all day?
Chewsday.

What is a duck's favourite food?
Cream quackers.

Who always makes Elmer laugh?
Duck – she's always
quacking jokes.

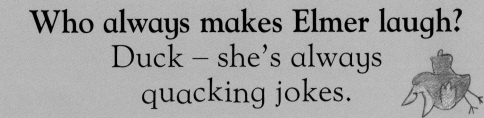

Why does Elmer have big ears?
So he can hear, of course.

What's yellow
and orange
and red
and pink
and purple
and blue
and green?

A rainbow.
(Elmer is also black and white.)

What's the last thing Elmer does
before he goes to sleep?
Close his eyes.

What do elephants talk in their sleep?
Mumbo Jumbo.